Anna and Aunt Alice's garden

Om KIDZ
An imprint of Om Books International

Om Kidz | Om Books International

Reprinted in 2023

Corporate & Editorial Office
A-12, Sector 64, Noida 201 301
Uttar Pradesh, India
Phone: +91 120 477 4100
Email: editorial@ombooks.com
Website: www.ombooksinternational.com

Sales Office
107, Ansari Road, Darya Ganj
New Delhi 110 002, India
Phone: +91 11 4000 9000
Email: sales@ombooks.com
Website: www.ombooks.com

ISBN: 978-93-52760-20-6

Printed in India

10 9 8 7 6 5 4 3 2

Anna and Aunt Alice's garden

Paste your photograph here

My name is

____

Anna loves **animals**.
She can spend hours **and** hours playing with them.

She has stuffed toys of **all** kinds of **animals** in her room.

There is **an alligator**;
an antelope; **and** even **a**
cuddly stuffed toy **ape**.

Summer holidays have just begun. **Anna** is going **away** to her **Aunt Alice's** house for the holidays.

She loves to go there, for **Aunt Alice** has **a** big, **airy** house on **a** farm garden.

Anna likes **Aunt Alice**.
She is **always** ready to
play with **Anna**.

She is **Anna's** favourite **aunt**.

Anna pretends **Aunt Alice's** farm garden is **a** magical forest with many **animals**.

They **all appear** when **Anna** visits them.

Anna pretends picnics with the **animals.**

She runs **around** with them. She feeds them **acorns and apricots**.

One day, she sits under **an acorn** tree munching **an apple** with squirrels running **around** her.

It is a warm **afternoon and Anna** is sleepy.

Anna falls **asleep** under the **acorn** tree. **All** of **a** sudden, she feels something crawling up her **arm**. "**Aaaah**!" she yells.

It is **a** little **ant**. **Anna** is not **afraid** of **ants**. But the **ant** is **afraid** of **Anna**.

"Oh! Please, don't hurt me!" the **ant** says in **a** little voice.

It is **a** talking **ant**!
Anna has never met one before. She is delighted.

"Of course, I will not hurt you," **Anna** says. "Would you like to share my **apple**?"

"Yes, please!" says the **ant**,
"I have lots of friends. **An apple** will give us food for days."
Anna gives **an apple** to the **ant**.

Suddenly **an army** of **ants appears**.
They crawl **all** over the **apple**.
As they feast on the **apple**,
an acorn falls on **Anna's** head.
Anna wakes up.

Anna looks **around** but there **are** no talking **ants** there. What **an** **amazing** dream! **Anna** has many more imaginary **adventures** with her **animal** friends.

Know your words

Naming words

Anna	apple	ape
animals	ant	acorn
alligator	aunt	Alice
antelope	army	

Describing words

airy	asleep	afraid
amazing		

Doing words

appear

Sight words

and	away	always
an	around	all
are	along	

Who will reach the apple?
Anna or the ants?

Colour the boxes with words starting with '**a**'.

pet	next	both	away	air
sweet	art	aunt	say	eat
dear	Anna	glue	cut	pay
empty	apple	Alice	tree	acorn

Find the given words in the wordsearch.

K	A	A	P	P	L	E	B
A	L	W	O	M	X	L	B
L	O	A	U	N	T	T	M
L	U	Y	Z	V	Z	Z	Q
O	D	A	R	O	U	N	D
W	A	R	T	C	E	U	F
W	S	A	S	J	V	P	X
B	Y	A	S	K	D	H	G

APPLE

ASK

AUNT

ALLOW

AWAY

AROUND